Santa's Moose

by Syd Hoff

An Early I CAN READ Book®

HARPER & ROW, PUBLISHERS

An Early I Can Read Book
is a registered trademark of
Harper & Row, Publishers, Inc.

Library of Congress Cataloging in Publication Data
Hoff, Sydney, date
    Santa's moose

    (An Early I can read book)
    SUMMARY: Milton, the big clumsy moose, helps Santa
one Christmas when his load is too heavy for the rein-
deer to pull.
    [1. Moose—Fiction.   2. Santa Claus—Fiction.
3. Christmas stories]   I. Title.
PZ7.H672San   [E]   78-22483
ISBN 0-06-022505-X
ISBN 0-06-022506-8 (lib. bdg.)
ISBN 0-06-444102-4 (pbk.)

For Liz Graves

It was winter in the forest.

"Soon Christmas will be here,"

said Milton the moose.

Birds landed

on his antlers

to rest,

then flew south.

The animals put holly leaves

on their nests and caves.

"We're on our way

to help Santa Claus,"

said eight little reindeer.

"That sounds like fun,"

said Milton.

He ran after the reindeer.

"May I please help
pull your sleigh?" asked Milton.

"I have never used a moose before,

but I'm willing

if you are," said Santa.

And across the sky they flew.

The eight little reindeer

liked Milton.

It was easy

to pull the heavy sleigh

with a big moose to help.

12

But Milton did not know

how to land on a roof.

KERPLUNK!

went Milton's big feet.

"Hush, you will wake everyone,"

said Santa.

13

Milton did not know

Santa went down chimneys alone.

He tried to go down too.

"You will get stuck," said Santa.

Milton waited

with the reindeer.

But he wanted to see

Santa fill the stockings

and put presents

around the Christmas tree.

He leaned over the roof

to peek,

and down he fell.

16

"I guess I should go home.

I guess I will never be good

at this," Milton said.

"Yes you will," said the reindeer.

"None of us were good
in the beginning."
"All it takes is practice,"
said Santa. "Please stay."

So Milton flew

all over the world

with Santa and

the eight little reindeer.

He learned to land on a roof.

He learned to stand still
and wait for Santa,
even when it took him
a long time.

At one house,

Santa let Milton

and the reindeer

stay on the ground.

24

Milton watched Santa

put presents

under the Christmas tree

and candy in the stockings.

"Christmas is the best time
of the year!" said Milton.
But the little reindeer were tired.
"We cannot go another step,"
they said.

"The load is so heavy this year!

But if we stop

there will be no presents

for millions of children."

"Do not stop!" cried Milton.

"I can pull the sleigh by myself."

Milton flew ahead.

The eight little reindeer

glided after him.

All the toys were delivered.

"Thank you, Milton,"

the reindeer said.

"We could not have done it

without you," said Santa.

"Will you help us next year?"

"Of course," said Milton.

28

"Merry Christmas!" said Santa.

"Merry Christmas!" cried the reindeer.

Santa and the reindeer

flew back to the North Pole.

Milton went back to the forest.
"Merry Christmas, everyone!"
he said.

He thought of Santa.

He thought of

the eight little reindeer.

He thought of next year,

when he would help them again.

"Joy to the world," he said,

"and peace on earth!"